♡ M. McKenna Bray

&

PIPPA

Pippa

ISBN 978-1-64003-112-8 (Hardcover)
ISBN 978-1-64003-111-1(Digital)

Covenant Books, Inc.
11661 Hwy 707
Murrells Inlet, SC 29576
www.covenantbooks.com

Pippa

McKenna Bray

There once was a girl
who traveled the world,
singing and singing away.

From a little ole mill,
on the top of a hill,
Pippa was her name.

Each morning began,
a guitar in her hand,
as she walked into town.

Every person along,
she sang them a song,
turning frowns upside down.

Pippa came across,
a child who was lost,
he was sad and all alone.

Pippa took his hand,
and soon, she began
to sing and a light was shown.

Far in the distance,
light made an appearance.
His parents followed the light.

They then heard a song
and even sang along.
They found him and smiled so bright.

Don't worry, my dear,
a light is near
that will guide you through your life.

Pippa saw a wave
from a girl who had prayed
for food and a shelter too.

Pippa only had
a guitar in her bag,
but she stayed and played a tune.

No food nor a home,
yet the song alone,
filled her up with joy and light.

She was so grateful,
joyful, and thankful.
It made her smile so bright.

Don't worry, my dear,
a light is near
that will guide you through your life.
There will be trouble,
you may even stumble,
but seek joy within the night.

Across the river,
a man with a shiver
was cold right down to the bone.

Pippa came to greet
the man and sing
a song to warm up his soul.

Some rain was in sight,
but the song was like
a warm blanket in disguise.

The man sang along.
He then felt so strong.
The warmth made him smile so bright.

Don't worry, my dear,
a light is near
that will guide you through your life.
There will be trouble,
you may even stumble,
but seek joy within the night.
A day can be cold,
but you should always know,
a song can warm up your soul.

Underneath a tree,
a boy scraped his knee,
then a tear streamed down his face.

He asked for some help.
Pippa came and knelt
beside him and sang away.

She was no doctor,
not a nurse either,
but sang, "You will be all right."

Music was healing,
the pain he was feeling,
he joined and smiled so bright.

Don't worry, my dear,
a light is near
that will guide you through your life.
There will be trouble,
you may even stumble,
but seek joy within the night.
A day can be cold,
but you should always know,
a song can warm up your soul.
There may be pain,
we may even complain,
but music can heal us all.

At the town square,
all gathered together,
and Pippa led them in song.

Each person she met,
all smiled and kept,
dancing and singing along.

Don't worry, my dear,
a light is near
that will guide you through your life.
There will be trouble,
you may even stumble,
but seek joy within the night.
A day can be cold,
but you should always know,
a song can warm up your soul.
There may be pain,
we may even complain,
but music can heal us all.

Each and every day,
and person on the way,
is important, so are you.

You should always know
there's a gift of your own
to share with those who are blue.

Remember to try
to use your gift to shine
a light to those all around.

Only one life we live,
so what can you give
to turn a frown upside down?

About the Author

McKenna Bray is a singer-songwriter and first-time children's author from Memphis, Tennessee.

Inspired by her own travels to Italy and the poetry of Robert Browning, Pippa came to life.

McKenna Bray enjoys painting, songwriting, and drinking coffee in pretty places.

CPSIA information can be obtained
at www.ICGtesting.com
Printed in the USA
LVHW07*0714221018
R14058500001B/R140585PG592469LVX1B/1/P